I MET AN ELK IN EDSON ONCE

Story by
Dave Kelly

Art by
Wes Tyrell

MacIntyre Purcell Publishing Inc.
194 Hospital Rd.
Lunenburg, Nova Scotia
B0J 2C0
(902) 640-3350

www.macintyrepurcell.com
info@macintyrepurcell.com

Printed and bound in Canada by Friesens

Design and layout Wes Tyrell

Library and Archives Canada Cataloguing in Publication

Kelly, Dave, 1964-, author   I met an elk in Edson once / written by Dave Kelly ; illustrated by Wes Tyrell.

Issued in print and electronic formats. ISBN 978-1-77276-031-6 (hardcover).--ISBN 978-1-77276-032-3 (HTML)

        I. Tyrell, Wes, 1964-, illustrator II. Title.

PS8621.E555I2 2017   jC813'.6   C2017-904921-6
C2017-904922-4

MacIntyre Purcell Publishing Inc. would like to acknowledge the financial support of the Government of Canada and the Nova Scotia Department of Tourism, Culture and Heritage.

I MET AN ELK IN EDSON ONCE

Story by
Dave Kelly

Art by
Wes Tyrell

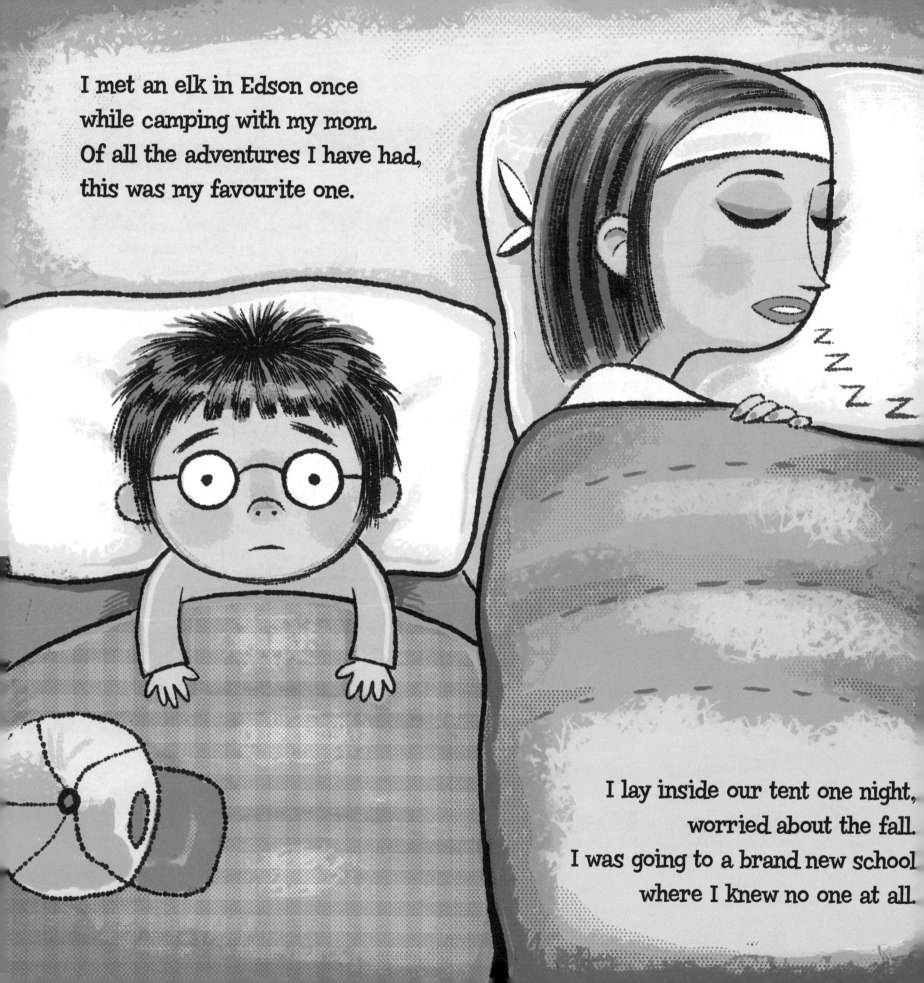

I met an elk in Edson once
while camping with my mom.
Of all the adventures I have had,
this was my favourite one.

I lay inside our tent one night,
worried about the fall.
I was going to a brand new school
where I knew no one at all.

I tried to rest and fall asleep.
I had almost closed my eyes,
when I heard a voice outside the tent say,
"These clothes are just my size."

I slowly pulled the tent flap up
and looked out in the night –
an elk had on my underwear
and they looked a little tight.

Then suddenly he noticed me
staring out at him.
He said, "I've got a problem,"
as he balanced on one limb.

"I need to ask a favour,
or maybe more, a dozen.
I want to wear your clothes and pretend
that I'm your ugly cousin."

I snuck out of the tent before
my mom woke up to see
that I was talking to an elk,
an elk dressed just like me.

He said, "I want to hitch a ride,"
then pulled my t-shirt on.
"I hope to find my uncle Todd -
it's been months since he's been gone."

"Well," I said, "it's nice to meet you but
some things seem rather odd –
like the fact that you can talk
and your uncle's name is Todd."

The elk said, "Yes, his name is Todd
and he left to find a home.
That's why I have to find him –
I don't like to be alone."

Then the elk walked up to me
and looked into my eyes:
"Will you take me in your car,
an elk in boy disguise?"

She said her name was Rusty
and I slowly realized
that he was actually a she –
I was a bit surprised

She said, "I don't have antlers -
that's something male elks do -
which is why I thought my head would fit
your clothes, and your car, too."

By this time the sun was rising,
and my mom woke up to see
her boy, an elk, and all my clothes
on Rusty and on me.

I sat her down and explained the deal,
while Rusty watched and ate.
Sometimes Mom freaks out a bit,
but this time she was great.

She thought awhile and then said, "Sure."
And that's how this came to be,
a trip around Alberta
with an elk, my mom and me.

We filled the car with all our stuff,
then Mom and I got in.
Rusty squeezed in beside me,
my rather ugly twin.

Our first stop was Jasper Park,
and the town that's called the same.
Everyone there said there are lots of elk,
but none that had a name.

We took their Skytram right to the top,
to look from up above.
We saw amazing scenery,
and views that my mom loved.

But no one there had heard of Todd,
so we drove to Banff and Lake Louise.
We hiked out on a glacier –
I thought that we might freeze.

Rusty asked some marmots,
some mountain goats and hares.
None of them were helpful,
So I said, "Let's ask some bears."

"Bear eat elk," frowned Rusty,
"so I have a little hunch
that if we walked up to a bear
all he'd see is lunch."

Rusty looked so sad and lost
that Mom and I agreed,
we had to have a bit of fun
at the Calgary Stampede.

The next day was the big parade,
so we got some chairs and sat.
No one noticed Rusty
in her boots and cowboy hat.

The parade was going fine until
the fireworks began.
I guess they sounded just like guns
'cause that's when Rusty ran.

I chased her through the parking lot
and tried to calm her down.
She was shaking in my shirt and shorts,
a full-on elk meltdown.

Next morning we packed up the car
and drove the Cowboy Trail,
a road through ranches, cows, and sky,
a western fairy tale.

Head-Smashed-In Buffalo Jump
was the next place that we found.
It's older than the pyramids,
it's also world-renowned.

Rusty walked out to the edge.
I knew her heart was thumping.
She said, "I guess it's pretty cool,
as long as you're not jumping!"

That's how people hunted then.
It was their way of life –
for food, for tools, for clothing
and heat on winter nights.

I said, "They ate some other things
including nuts and plants."
Rusty said, "They also used
my great grandparents for pants."

Morning came and we drove east,
and the prairie sky expanded
We searched for Rusty's uncle Todd
but came up empty-handed.

We went to towns like Fort Macleod,
and Lethbridge and through Brooks.
Everyone smiled at me and Mom
but gave Rusty some funny looks.

JAPANESE-CANADIAN
CULTURAL CENTRE

We drove until the prairie changed,
that sunny afternoon,
to a place they call the Badlands,
like walking on the moon.

We saw these things called hoodoos,
which are rocks that stand up tall,
and then The Royal Tyrrell Museum,
the greatest place of all.

The place is packed with dinosaurs
and by T-Rex number five,
Rusty said, "I gotta go
before this one comes alive!"

That evening Mom looked through her books
to find where elk might be;
while Rusty asked about my life,
my friends and family.

I said, "Alberta's new for us,
it's just my mom and me.
We moved here and we're camping
to see what we could see."

Then suddenly my mom stood up –
"I've got it! Hey, you two!
There's a place called Elk Island National Park
and it's full of elk like you!"

Rusty jumped up from her seat
and made an elky sound.
She said, "I know my uncle's there!"
"Now, now," Mom said, "settle down."

They were both so happy
Rusty almost lost her head!
I tried to smile and join the fun
but I just felt sad instead.

I said to Rusty and to Mom,
"I finally found a friend
I know that Rusty has to go
but I'm sad it has to end."

BUMP

"Well," said Mom, "how about
before we say goodbye,
we try a massive waterpark
with a roof across the sky?"

So we drove to Edmonton.
Mom took us to the Mall.
We marched right to the Waterpark,
the biggest one of all.

It had the greatest waterslides
that I had ever seen.
All day long my friend and I
just laughed and slid and screamed.

SPLOOSH!

We slowly drove out east of town
to a campsite in the dark.
Rusty jumped out of the car
at Elk Island National Park.

I lay down in my sleeping bag,
and heard Mom start to snore.
Then I heard some rustling...
just like I'd heard before.

Rusty stepped into the light,
then another elk stepped out.
I said, "You must be Uncle Todd."
He answered, "Without a doubt."

Rusty returned my shirt and pants
and hats and boots and socks.
"I loved this trip," she said to me,
this elk who walks and talks.

"So when you start your school this fall -
as lonely as can be -
remember an elk in underwear,
and that you're never far from me."

I said, "You keep the underwear.
I think they look good on you.
And now that I think of it,
Uncle Todd can have some too."

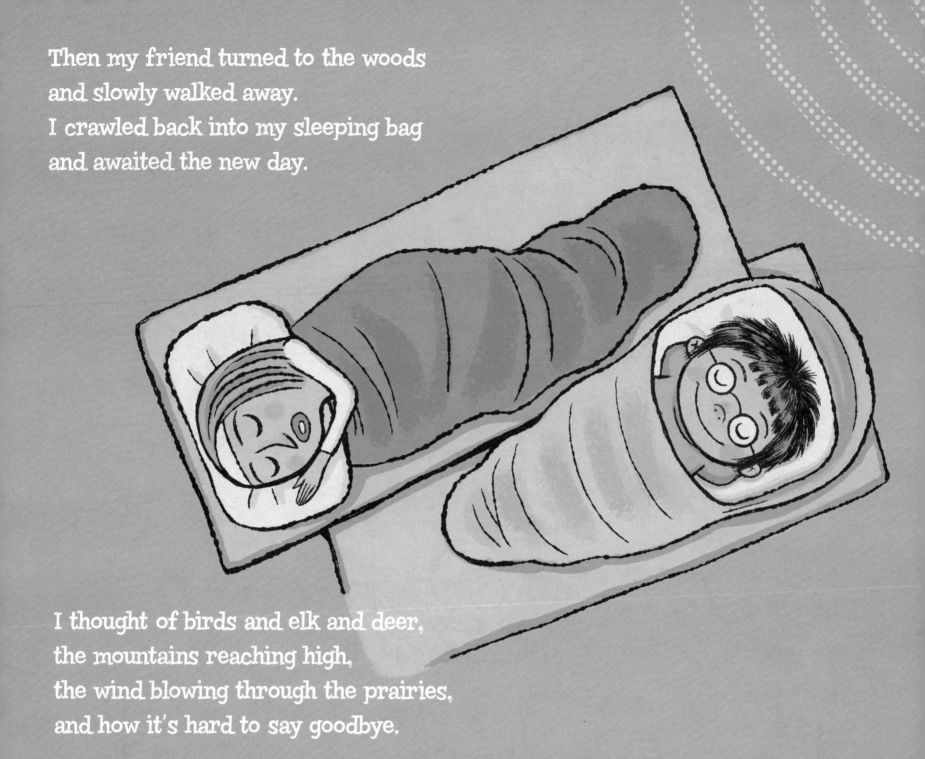

Then my friend turned to the woods
and slowly walked away.
I crawled back into my sleeping bag
and awaited the new day.

I thought of birds and elk and deer,
the mountains reaching high,
the wind blowing through the prairies,
and how it's hard to say goodbye.

I met an elk in Edson once.
I was camping with my mom.
Of all the adventures I have had,
this was my favourite one.